BUTTONS

Copyright © 2003 by Michael Neugebauer Verlag,
an imprint of Nord-Süd Verlag AG, Gossau Zürich, Switzerland
First published in Switzerland under the title *Grosser Bär & kleiner Bär*.
English translation copyright © 2004 by North-South Books Inc., New York
All rights reserved. No part of this book may be reproduced or utilized
in any form or by any means, electronic or mechanical, including
photocopying, recording, or any information storage and retrieval system,
without permission in writing from the publisher.
First published in the United States, Great Britain, Canada,
Australia, and New Zealand in 2004 by North-South Books,
an imprint of Nord-Süd Verlag AG, Gossau Zürich, Switzerland.
Distributed in the United States by North-South Books Inc., New York.
Library of Congress Cataloging-in-Publication Data is available.
A CIP catalogue record for this book is available from The British Library.
ISBN 0-7358-1883-5 (trade edition) 10 9 8 7 6 5 4 3 2 1
ISBN 0-7358-1884-3 (library edition) 10 9 8 7 6 5 4 3 2 1
Printed in Italy

SATOSHI ITAYA

AND **BO**

TRANSLATED BY MARIANNE MARTENS

A MICHAEL NEUGEBAUER BOOK
NORTH-SOUTH BOOKS NEW YORK / LONDON

Buttons was angry—really, really angry. Bo, his crybaby brother, was howling again. Mother will give Bo whatever he wants, as usual, thought Buttons. And sure enough, Mother handed Buttons's red car to Bo.

"That's *my* car!" yelled Buttons.

"Oh, come now, let him play with it for a while," said Mother. "He's just a little bear."

He sure is a big howler for such a little bear, Buttons thought huffily. He picked up Bo's toy box and threw all the toys around the room.

Bo looked at him, surprised.

"There!" said Buttons. "Now you have something to cry about." He stuck out his tongue and marched out of the house.

Outside, Buttons felt better right away. I'll go over to the meadow, he thought. Suddenly he heard the pitter-patter of little bear steps behind him.

"Buttons, Buttons, wait for me!"

"Oh no!" said Buttons. "You are *not* coming with me."

Little Bo reached for Buttons's paw. "Please?"
"No," said Buttons. "I don't want you along.
Go home to Mother, you little crybaby."
Buttons stomped off without looking back.

But when Buttons got to the meadow, Bo was still behind him. Buttons pretended to ignore him.

He picked the biggest dandelions and blew. Silver parachutes floated gently in the air. Bo picked a dandelion, too, and blew on it. The parachutes flew up and tickled him in the nose. *Aaa-tchooo!* sneezed Bo.

Buttons grinned smugly. Bo couldn't even blow dandelions.

Buttons walked on. Bo followed right behind. When Buttons got to the stream he took a running start and leaped to the other side. "Hah!" he said to himself. "Let's see Bo do that! He's going to get his paws wet and then he'll run home to Mother."
But Bo looked around carefully and found a couple of big rocks to use for steps. He made it safely to the other side, nice and dry.

Buttons walked on, and soon he was at the edge of the forest. Bo stayed right behind him. "Okay, you little baby bear, watch this!" Buttons said to himself. He climbed over high stones, crept through scratchy bushes, and balanced on a giant tree trunk.

"Phew! I made it!" said Buttons, feeling very pleased with himself. "Bet you can't do that!"

Bo didn't dare try. Carefully, he walked around the big rocks and hedges and tree trunks, until he was right behind his brother again.

"I can't stand it!" Buttons cried. He stomped
off deeper and deeper into the forest.
Bo stayed right on his heels. It grew
darker and darker, and suddenly Buttons
realized that he was lost.
Buttons looked around nervously. The
forest was full of strange creaking and
crunching sounds. And there were such
eerie lights twinkling everywhere. It
was very spooky.

"I bet you're really scared now," said Buttons, his voice shaking. But Bo shook his head. "Of course not! You're here!"

"That's right," said Buttons bravely, and he gave Bo a hug. Bo snuggled against his brother, as happy as could be. But Buttons was worried.

How were they going to find their way back home? Mother and Father Bear would be upset. And maybe the forest was haunted!

Bo wasn't the least bit concerned. "What
do you want to play now?" he asked.
"*What?*" said Buttons, confused. And then he
had a brilliant idea. "Let's play that you're a
little bear who is lost in the forest and you're
scared so you start to howl for your mother.
You know how good you are at howling!"

"Oh, yes I am!" Bo glowed. Then he howled and wailed and cried and screamed so loudly that the sound carried through the forest and out the other side. Buttons helped a little too. Soon they saw two big lights coming closer and closer.

The lights belonged to Mother and Father! They hugged
Buttons and Bo. "I'm so glad that Bo is such a good howler,"
said Mother. "We could hear you from far, far away."
Buttons nodded, reached for Bo's paw, and held it all
the way home.